Dedicated in loving memory to my mom, Brenda "GiGi" Dolina. She was the biggest supporter on my journey through Autism. She was able to read most of my stories while she was still with us, and that makes me smile. Thank you for always inspiring me to complete my writing, Mom. You are loved and missed.

www.mascotbooks.com

Adventures With Big E: Help With Hygiene

For more information, please contact:
Mascot Books
620 Herndon Parkway, Suite 320
Herndon, VA 20170
info@mascotbooks.com

Library of Congress Control Number: 2018914765

CPSIA Code: PRT0319A
ISBN-13: 978-1-64307-229-6

Printed in the United States

Adventures With Big E

Help With Hygiene

Jacqualine Folks

illustrated by Yasu Matsuoka

Big E Brushes His Teeth

My name is Ethan. My friends call me Big E. Come along on a journey with me. Today we will be learning how to brush our teeth.

This is what we need to brush our teeth:

Floss

Cup

Toothbrush

Sink

Toothpaste

These things make brushing my teeth hard for me. The flavor of the toothpaste tastes yucky. The touch of the toothbrush feels funny on my teeth and gums. I don't like how the floss feels tight and rubs my gums. But I still need to brush my teeth.

I also need to do everything in the right order. All of the steps confuse me, but my mom is here to help. She even made pictures of each step that I can follow.

3.

4.

5.

6.

7.

When I started out, my mom brushed my teeth for me. Then she helped with her hand over my hand. Then she let me try all by myself. At first I wasn't very good. I needed help. Help is okay as long as you keep trying.

I kept trying and trying, and each time I got better until I could do it all by myself. Practice makes perfect! You can do it!

Thank you for coming on this journey with me. Now we can brush our teeth! You will always learn to be brave and keep trying with your new friend Big E.

Big E Takes a Bath

My name is Ethan. My friends call me Big E. Come along on a journey with me. Today we will be learning how to take a bath.

There are so many things to remember at bath time.
This is what we need:

- Soap

- Shampoo

- Rinse cup

- Towel

- Don't forget your favorite bath toys!

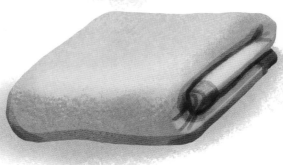

It's time to get in the water. Water can be very scary. It is loud when it is on and I do not like it on my face or in my ears. Sometimes I wear a bath hat and earplugs to help. Even though I am a little scared, I get in.

The water feels like a warm hug and the bubbles help me wash my body and hair.

My mom makes bath time lots of fun. She makes sure all of my ocean friends are in the tub with me. Sometimes she even makes the bath water glow! My mom also makes sure my loofa is sudsy so I can clean every finger and every toe. Remember, if you stay calm and wash really fast, you can play with your favorite bath toys longer!

I did it!

Bath time is over. I am fresh and clean. I dry off with my towel. Sometimes I don't like how the towel feels on my skin, but I know I can't stay wet forever. Bath time wasn't that scary after all, and I even had fun! You can too!

Thank you for coming on this journey with me. Now we can take a bath! You will always learn to be brave and keep trying with your new friend Big E.

Big E
Goes Potty

My name is Ethan. My friends call me Big E. Come along on a journey with me. Today we will be learning how to go potty.

I don't always remember to tell my mom when I need to go potty, but she always remembers to ask me if I have to go. Even if I don't feel like I have to potty when she asks, I always try.

My mom posted pictures all around the potty to help me remember all of the steps. I look at them every time I go. Always remember to wash your hands!

Potty training can be hard, but my mom helps make it fun. We play lots of potty games!

Sometimes my silly mom puts Cheerios in the potty. It is so much fun to try and potty in the circles.

Sometimes she puts food coloring in the potty. It is so much fun to potty on the colors and watch them spread out.

I love playing my mom's fun games every time I go to the potty.

Going poop isn't as easy as going pee-pee, but we still make it fun. We sing songs. We look at books. We even play toys. But I have to remember to concentrate and try to go poop.

If I try my best my mom gives me a reward. Sometimes I get a hug. Sometimes she sings me a song. Sometimes I get to pick a special treat. Make sure you try as hard as you can and maybe you'll get a reward too. You can do it!

Thank you for coming on this journey with me. Now we can go potty! You will always learn to be brave and keep trying with your new friend Big E.

Big E Gets a Haircut

My name is Ethan. My friends call me Big E. Come along on a journey with me. Today we will be learning how to be brave while getting a haircut.

I do not like haircuts. The scissors look scary. The chair is so big. The clippers are so loud as they buzz buzz around my head. I do not like the itchy hair that falls on me.

But there are things I can do to make haircuts less scary!

The first thing I can do is get to know my barber. My barber's name is Rex. He is cool! He even gives me magic sunglasses to wear that make the scissors look friendlier!

I can sit on my mom or dad's lap to feel safe in the big chair. Sometimes we read a book or play a game in the chair. That helps me take my mind off how nervous I am.

I also like to wear earplugs so the clippers sound less scary and the hair stays out of my ears. And we always bring an extra shirt for me to change into. That way, I don't have itchy hair all over me.

If I am brave during my haircut, I get a reward. I also look great with my new haircut, which makes it all worth it. You can look great too if you're brave! You can do it!

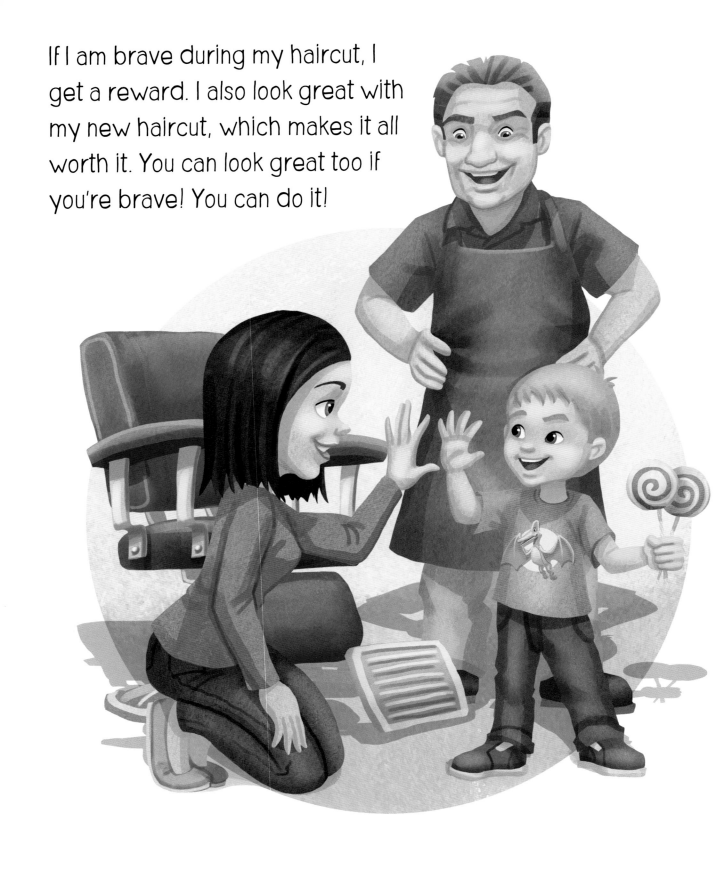

Thank you for coming on this journey with me. Now we can be brave during our haircuts! You will always learn to be brave and keep trying with your new friend Big E.

Big E Gets Dressed

My name is Ethan. My friends call me Big E. Come along on a journey with me. Today we will be learning how to get dressed.

Clothes feel itchy and heavy. I don't like to wear them. When my mom wakes me up, I want to stay in my comfy jammies all day. But my mom says I have to get dressed.

Cool Clothes
Warm Clothes

Picking out clothes can be a little hard for me. Before I pick them out, I need to remember to check the weather. If it's hot outside, I need to wear cool clothes. If it's cold outside, I need to wear warm clothes.

My mom put pictures on my dresser so it's easy for me to find my clothes. Once I find them, my parents can help me learn front and back.

Front

Back

Sometimes the tags
on the clothes bother me.

Sometimes the materials
feel funny on my skin.

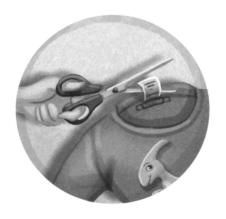

If either of those things happen,
I tell my parents and they cut off
the tag or find another material that
doesn't bother me.

Before long, I am all dressed and ready for the day. If I keep practicing every day, I'll be able to get dressed all on my own. You can too!

Thank you for coming on this journey with me. Now we know how to get dressed! You will always learn to be brave and keep trying with your new friend Big E.

A Note from the Author

I would like to thank you all for purchasing *Adventures With Big E: Help With Hygiene*. I started writing these social stories for my son to offset the extremely high cost of therapy services for kids with Autism. In each story are methods I used that may help you along your journey with your child.

When my son was younger, hygiene was always an issue. It took us many years to master proper personal care. Ethan just turned 18 and it was only recently that he has been able to complete all of the topics in this book independently. Naturally, he mastered certain areas over the years, but he is now 100% independent, even completing these tasks without verbal prompts.

The most important thing to remember while parenting your child with Autism is that you are doing your very best! These methods that were successful for Ethan and I may not work for every child, but my hope is that adding stories with repetition and a friendly face to these methods will strengthen them so they can apply to more children. I longed for a resource like this when I was teaching my son and I am glad to be able to share this with you.

Ethan has been my biggest inspiration and teacher in life. He has made me a better person and I hope he can inspire millions of kids through his stories.

– Jacqualine Folks

Thank you to Eudora ACES (Autism Community Education and Support) for their grant toward illustrating this book.

@Eudora ACES

About the Author

Jacqualine "Jacqui" Folks is an author who lives in Eudora, Kansas, with her husband, Mike. She is a busy mother of three sons: Bret, Ethan, and Garrett.

In 2003 Jacqui's middle son, Ethan, was diagnosed with Autism. His diagnosis came at a time when resources for Autism were scarce, so Jacqui found herself on a journey of self-education to enrich the life of her child. Though she still found time to support her other sons on the soccer field, most of her time was spent in libraries learning all she could about Autism education, therapies, and advocacy.

In 2005 Jacqui started a support group for parents in her local community. Several years later, the ladies she met through that journey joined forces and co-founded the Eudora ACES (Autism Community Education and Support). ACES is a successful non-profit organization dedicated to helping other families with their journey through Autism and supplying necessary equipment and resources for special education classes in their school district.

Adventures With Big E: Help With Hygiene is Jacqui's first children's book.